GILBERT IN DEEP

For Andy and Rob, with loads of love
J.C.
For Aidan and Joely
C.F.

The great white shark is one of the supreme predators of the ocean. White sharks can grow to about 20 feet long (6 meters), the females being a little bigger than the males, and can weigh over 3 tons. But, in spite of their size, white sharks can leap clear out of the water!

White sharks are found in parts of the Pacific, Atlantic and Indian Oceans, and in the Mediterranean Sea. Because of their rarity and secretive behavior, there is much we do not know about great white sharks.

In warmer waters sharks are often accompanied by a small fish called a remora. Remoras can have a close relationship with a shark, scavenging for leftover food and nibbling off shrimp-like parasites that grow on the shark's body. The remora may stay with a single shark for a while, hitching a lift by sticking to the shark's underside with a special sucker found on its head.

The Shark Trust is the conservation agency dedicated to the study, management and conservation of sharks. To find out more about sharks, become a member, or adopt a shark like Gilbert, visit www.sharktrust.org.

STERLING CHILDREN'S BOOKS and the distinctive Sterling Children's Books logo are trademarks of Sterling Publishing Co., Inc.

Text © 2007 by Jane Clarke
Illustrations © 2007 by Charles Fuge

Paperback edition published in 2016.
Previously published by Sterling Publishing, Co., Inc. in a different format in 2007.
Published by arrangement with Simon & Schuster UK Ltd.

ISBN 978-1-4549-2117-2

Distributed in Canada by Sterling Publishing
c/o Canadian Manda Group, 664 Annette Street
Toronto, Ontario, Canada M6S 2C8

For information about custom editions, special sales, and premium and corporate purchases, please contact Sterling Special Sales at 800-805-5489 or specialsales@sterlingpublishing.com.

Manufactured in China
Lot #:
2 4 6 8 10 9 7 5 3 1
07/16

www.sterlingpublishing.com

GILBERT IN DEEP

Jane Clarke & Charles Fuge

STERLING CHILDREN'S BOOKS
New York

Gilbert the great white shark loved
to play hide-and-seek with Rita Remora.

But they already knew all the nooks
and crannies in the coral reef,
and all the hiding places in the Wreck.

So one day, after school, Gilbert asked his mother,
"Mom, can we go and play hide-and-seek
on the other side of the reef?"

"Go ahead," Mom said. "But be sure
to be back before sunset. And don't
go over the Edge!"

Gilbert and Rita swam off happily.

The sea was rough on the other side of the reef.
When Gilbert hid in the surging surf,
Rita was tumbled and tossed by the waves.
And when Rita hid in the swirling seaweed,
Gilbert got terribly tangled.

"I'm tired of playing hide-and-seek," sighed Gilbert.
"Let's swim off the Edge, and play hide-and-*deep!*"
"Your mom told us not to," warned Rita. "She'll go
off the deep end!"
"She won't know, as long as we're back before sunset,"
Gilbert grinned. He was ready for an adventure.

The edge of the reef dropped away into inky darkness.

"It's dark in the Deep," Gilbert said, peering over the Edge.
"You're not scared of the dark, are you?" asked Rita.
"Me? Scared?" gulped Gilbert. "Great white sharks are *fearless!*"

And they dove off the Edge together.

Above them, pale rays of watery sunshine
silhouetted a shimmering shadow.

"It's a ghost whale!" Rita froze in her fins.
"Boo!" Gilbert shouted.

The huge shadow broke up into glittering rainbows.
"It's only cuttlefish." Gilbert grinned at Rita.
"There's nothing to be afraid of."

Down and down they dove through
the deep, dark ocean.

They stopped at the entrance to a cave.
"I can't see a thing in here!" said Gilbert. "It's the perfect
place to play hide-and-deep. My turn to hide!"
He took a deep breath and swam in.
Rita covered her eyes with her fins and began to count to ten.

Whump!
Gilbert bumped into a giant empty clamshell.
He wriggled inside.

"8…9…10…
Ready or not, here I come!" Rita
called in a wobbly voice.

Gilbert peeked out of the clamshell.

A ghostly green light was glowing
in the darkness.
The light bobbed closer.
Gilbert's heart beat faster.
The light bobbed past the clamshell.
It was bobbing toward Rita!

Then the light went out.

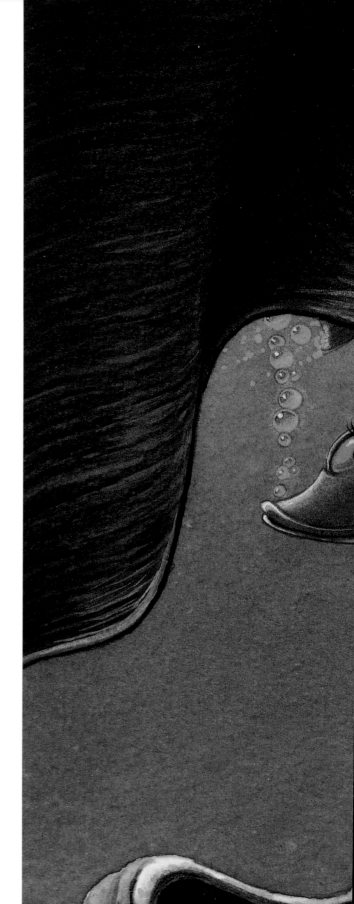

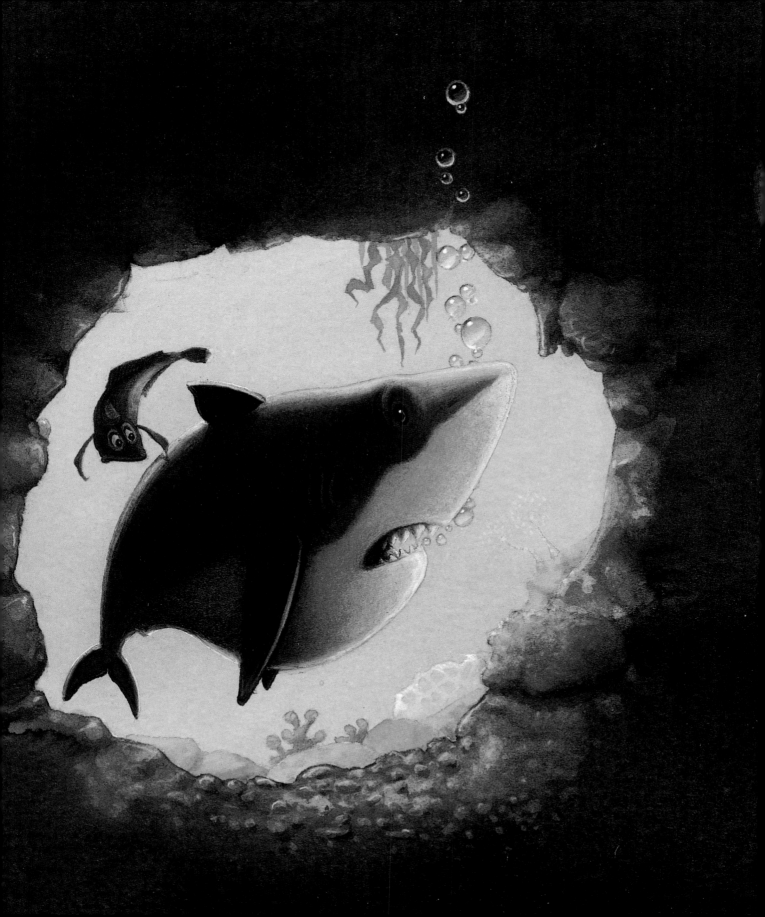

Gilbert's tummy did a somersault. He squeezed out of his hiding place. "R-R-R-Rita? Where are you?"

"Gilbert!" Rita squealed. "There's a green-eyed monster in this cave!" Gilbert's teeth began to chatter.

"I'm not a monster!" said a gravelly voice. "I'm an angler fish. My name is Glowanna."

"I . . . I can't see you," Gilbert stammered. "It's much too dark."

"Why didn't you say so?" said Glowanna. "Ready . . . set . . .

. . . glow!"

The cave was bathed in an eerie green light.
"Ahhh!" Gilbert gasped.

"Ahhh!" Glowanna and her friends shrieked.
They took one look at Gilbert's teeth and
leaped into each other's fins.

Rita crept back to Gilbert's side.
Gilbert took a deep breath.
"H-hello, G-Glowanna," he spluttered.
"There's no need to be scared," said Glowanna.
"Me? Scared?" gulped Gilbert.
"Great white sharks are *fearless!*"

Rita nudged Gilbert nervously. "We'd better get back before your mom finds out we went over the Edge."

"Come up and play hide-and-seek with us sometime, Glowanna." said Gilbert in his bravest voice.

"I'm not going up there!" Glowanna gasped. "All *sorts* of scary things live in the light!"

Gilbert swam out of the cave.
"That's not the way we came!" called Rita.

But Gilbert was already swimming up
toward the rays of the setting sun.
Rita raced to catch up with him.

All around them, seaweed swayed and spooky shadows swirled. Everything looked wrong.

"S-stick close to me, R-Rita," stammered Gilbert.

Moonlight began to filter into the deep blue ocean. Above them, a huge, silvery moonshadow was creeping along the Edge. A moonshadow with beady eyes and ferocious teeth. It crept closer, and closer, and . . .

"Gilbert! Get up here this minute!" Gilbert's mother thundered.
"You're in deep trouble!"
Gilbert and Rita looked at each other.
"Uh-oh!" they gulped.

"I told you not to go over the Edge!" Mom said.
"You are not to go out of my sight until
I am sure that I can trust you again!"

Gilbert's fins drooped. "S-s-sorry, Mom,"
he whispered. "We won't do it again!"

Gilbert's mother hugged him tightly.
"Well, thank goodness I found you!
I was scared you were lost in the Deep," she said.
"I was a little scared, too." admitted Gilbert.

"You said great white sharks were *fearless!*"

Rita reminded him.

In the moonlit ocean, Gilbert the great white shark
looked up at his mother and smiled a shaky, sharky smile.

"We *are* fearless," Gilbert said. "*Most* of the time."

The End